CHAPTER 1
Homesick in Beijing

"I miss Grandpa Harry's waffles," Ella Briar said with a pout.

"I miss the blueberry muffins from Petunia Bakery," her brother, Ethan, added.

The twins frowned at their plates, which were piled high with fried rice, pickled vegetables, and some foods they didn't recognize. The Briar

family was having breakfast at their hotel, the Beijing Imperial. The large dining room was decorated with red and gold furniture and paintings of swirly dragons.

"But, kids, we're having an eating adventure!" their dad, Andrew, said as he reached for his chopsticks. "Check out those delicious-looking *bao*!"

"Our neighbor Mrs. Chen used to make *bao* when I was growing up," their mom, Josephine, said with a smile. "My favorites were the ones with sweet beans in them. They tasted like little cakes!"

Ella picked up a *bao* and bit into it carefully. The steamed bun was warm and soft on the outside and filled with sweet barbecued meat inside. It was actually really good.

She still missed Grandpa Harry's waffles, though. He always decorated them with chocolate-chip smiley faces. Ella missed everything and everyone back in Brookeston. She knew Ethan did too.

The Briars had been traveling around the world for more than a month now. The reason for their big trip was Mrs. Briar's job. The *Brookeston Times* newspaper had hired her to write a travel column, Journeys with Jo!

They had already visited two cities in Europe: Venice, Italy, and Paris, France. After that, they had moved on to Shanghai, China. And just yesterday, they had arrived in Beijing, the capital of China.

"So what are we doing today?" Ethan asked. He stuck his chopsticks in his brown hair and made them stand up like antennas. Ella giggled. Her brother looked like a bug!

Mrs. Briar scrolled through her cell phone. "I just got an e-mail from my editor. He wants me to interview some people over at the National Art

Museum. I'm afraid I'll be tied up until dinnertime."

Ella's face fell. So did Ethan's. That was another thing they missed—spending time with their mom. She was always busy writing or doing research for her column. The twins were mostly with their dad, either sightseeing or having their homeschooling lessons.

Mrs. Briar reached across the table to squeeze their hands. "I'm sorry I can't be with you guys today. But guess what? The four of us are doing something really special tomorrow!"

Ella perked up. "What is it?"

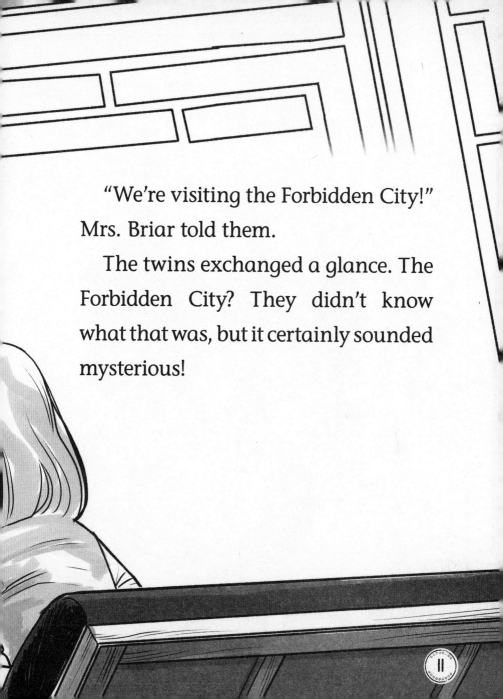

"We're visiting the Forbidden City!" Mrs. Briar told them.

The twins exchanged a glance. The Forbidden City? They didn't know what that was, but it certainly sounded mysterious!

CHAPTER 2

A New Mystery

That night in their hotel room, Ethan and Ella decided to check their e-mail before going to sleep. It was early for bedtime, but they were tired from spending the day working on math and science lessons with their dad. Second grade was hard!

The twins plopped down on Ethan's bed and placed the laptop between

them. Ethan wore his dinosaur pajamas. Ella's pajamas had hearts on them. Mr. and Mrs. Briar were in the next room, talking and drinking tea.

Ethan signed on to their account. There was an e-mail from Ethan's best friend, Theo. Theo had written that their soccer team, the Brookeston Boomers, had won their last match. There was another e-mail from Ella's best friend, Hannah, with a new poem for their poetry club.

There was a third e-mail, from Grandpa Harry. The twins opened it eagerly.

To: ethanella@eemail.com

From: gpaharry@eemail.com

Subject: The Three Dragons

Hello, my dears. *Huānyíng lai Beijing!* (That means "Welcome to Beijing!" in Mandarin.)

I hear that you are visiting the Forbidden City tomorrow. The Forbidden City was the emperor's palace for hundreds of years. It is called that because no one could enter or leave the palace grounds without the emperor's permission. (The word "forbidden" means "not allowed.")

These days, the Forbidden City is a tourist site. While you are there, be sure to go to the Imperial Garden. There you will find paths decorated with beautiful statues of animals. These statues are symbols for different things. (In Chinese culture, elephants symbolize strength; tigers symbolize courage; rabbits symbolize hope; grasshoppers symbolize wisdom, and so on.)

Perhaps you could look for the path that has my favorite statue. It's of three dragons. The dragons are red, green, and purple, and they symbolize good luck. In fact, I had some very good luck after I came across those dragons! Here is a clue: They are near the old pine tree.

Lots of love,

Grandpa Harry

Ella looked up at Ethan, her brown eyes twinkling. "A new mystery!" she exclaimed.

Ethan nodded. He and Ella loved solving mysteries. Back in Brookeston, they'd found Ethan's missing gold coin. It had been a going-away present from Grandpa Harry. In Venice, they'd tracked down a stolen gondola.

And in Paris, they had helped to catch a painting thief.

Ella reached across Ethan to grab something from the nightstand.

"Hey, you're squishing me!" Ethan complained.

"Sorry! I needed these." Ella held up her purple notebook and a pen.

"What for?" Ethan asked.

"To write down some notes about our new mystery!" Ella replied.

The notebook had been Ella's

going-away present from Grandpa Harry. Ethan watched as his sister wrote:

Go to the Imperial Garden in the Forbidden City.

Find the old pine tree.

Find the path with three dragons. The dragons are red, green, and purple.

dragons = good luck

elephants = strength

tigers = courage

rabbits = hope

grasshoppers = wisdom

Ella closed the notebook and hugged it to her chest. "I can't wait for tomorrow!"

"Let's go to sleep! That way, tomorrow will happen faster," Ethan said with a grin.

CHAPTER 3

The Forbidden City

The next morning, the Briar family walked over to the Forbidden City. It was only a few blocks from their hotel.

Though she was still a little home-sick, Ella liked Beijing. It was both an old and a new city. Tall, modern sky-scrapers stood next to ancient temples. The streets bustled with cars, bicycles, and rickshaws, which were passenger carts drawn by bikes. Farmers sold fresh fruit on the sidewalks out of baskets that hung from bamboo poles.

Soon enough, the Briars reached the Forbidden City. It was surrounded by a moat. Ethan had read about moats in his books about ancient kingdoms. He never thought he'd see a real one, though!

"Let's play knights!" he suggested.

The twins pretended to ride on horseback across the moat bridge. They swung invisible swords through the air. Mr. Briar followed them with

his video camera while Mrs. Briar took photos.

The four of them made their way to the main entrance. After getting their tickets, they found themselves in a large square crowded with tourists.

Mr. Briar unfolded his pocket map and studied it. "The Hall of Supreme Harmony is straight ahead," he said, pointing. "I thought we could start there."

"Is harmony the thing we studied in music class?" Ethan asked.

"Yes, but in music, harmony means notes sounding good together. In this case, harmony means people getting along well together," Mr. Briar explained.

"Everything in the Forbidden City has a poetic name," Mrs. Briar remarked. "The Hall of Supreme Harmony . . . the Pavilion of Ever-lasting Spring . . ."

Ella repeated the names under her breath. They were so pretty! She wondered if she and Ethan should name their tree house

back in Brookeston. *The Tree House of Supreme Fun . . . The Tree House of Everlasting Snacks . . .*

Mr. Briar led the way through a gate that was guarded by two bronze lions. Just beyond was the Hall of Supreme

Harmony. It was an enormous building with red pillars and marble stairs.

Inside, a woman led a group of tourists. She was speaking English. Mrs. Briar went over and spoke to her.

"The tour guide said we could join her group!" Mrs. Briar explained when she came back. "This way, we can get

the true inside scoop on the Forbidden City."

"Sounds wonderful!" Mr. Briar said excitedly. He was a history professor, and he loved to learn about anything and everything.

Mrs. Briar slipped her sunglasses into her purse and turned to the twins.

"Stay close to us. Our guide said that there are more than nine hundred buildings in the Forbidden City—and more than eight thousand rooms."

Nine hundred buildings? Eight thousand rooms?

"Okay!" Ella promised.

Ethan nodded quickly.

"The Hall of Supreme Harmony is more than six hundred years old," the tour guide explained to the group as she led them into a large room. Colorful animal designs covered the fancy ceiling. "The emperor used to hold important meetings here. There were royal weddings, birthdays, and other celebrations here too. The last emperor of China was named Puyi," the tour guide went on. "He became the emperor when he was just two years old."

Ethan blinked. A two-year-old emperor? How was that even possible?

Just then, someone bumped up against Ella, which made her drop her bag. She bent down to get it—and noticed something odd. The man in front of her had a piece of paper stuck to his shoe.

Ella pointed it out to Ethan. "Maybe it's toilet paper!" Ethan whispered. The twins giggled quietly.

As the man moved away, the paper fluttered loose. But it wasn't toilet paper. It almost looked like a map!

Ella picked it up. It *was* a map. It was yellow and crinkly and looked old. There were strange symbols on it.

"Is it a map of Beijing?" Ethan asked.

"I don't know. It's not like the one Dad got from the hotel." Ella studied the map more closely. "This looks like a gate with two lions. Didn't we go through a gate like that?"

"Yeah, we did! Maybe it's a map of the Forbidden City?" Ethan guessed.

The twins tried to make out the other symbols. The room suddenly seemed quiet.

Ethan and Ella glanced up. Their tour group was gone. And so were their parents!

CHAPTER 4

Lost!

"Where did they go?" Ella cried out.

Ethan did a three-sixty spin, which was one of his favorite soccer moves. It allowed him to scan the whole room very quickly.

There were four doors leading out. Each door was decorated with identical designs.

Ethan pointed to the closest one

and said, "Let's try that way!"

"Okay," Ella agreed. She tucked the map carefully into her messenger bag, and the twins hurried to the door.

On the other side was a small room full of statues, sculptures, and paintings. A couple admired a bronze tortoise.

"Excuse me! Did you see our tour

group?" Ella asked them breathlessly. "Our mom and dad were with them. Our mother has blond hair. Our father is really tall. He has brown hair and glasses."

The woman shook her head. The man said something in Chinese.

"I guess they don't speak English," Ethan said to Ella.

"Thank you, anyway," Ella told the couple. *"Xièxie!"*

The man and woman smiled and nodded.

"Um, what did you just say to them?" Ethan asked Ella curiously.

"I said 'thank you' in Chinese," Ella replied.

"When did you learn Chinese?!" Ethan asked.

"Dad taught us

some phrases in Shanghai, remember? I guess you weren't paying attention," Ella teased.

"I was too!" Ethan snapped. Actually, he'd been sneaking peeks at his comic books during that lesson. "Come on. Let's keep going. We have to find Mom and Dad."

The twins went to the next room . . . and the next . . . and the next.

But there was no sign of their tour

group or their parents anywhere.

"Weren't we just here?" Ella asked when they reached yet another room.

"Were we?" Ethan glanced around. It was a small room full of statues, sculptures, and paintings. All the rooms looked alike!

"Now what?" Ella said, frustrated.

Ethan shrugged. "I'm not sure. How do you say 'we're lost' in Chinese?"

Ella reached into her bag and pulled out the crinkly old map. "I know! Let's use this map to find that garden Grandpa Harry told us about," she suggested. "He said the dragon path

there was good luck. Maybe we'll have some good luck, too, and find Mom and Dad afterward!"

"I like that plan. Does the map have any garden symbols on it?" Ethan asked.

Ella held the map up to the light. She and Ethan went over it carefully.

"What about this?" Ethan pointed to a symbol that looked like a tree. "Hey, wait a second. Didn't Grandpa Harry say something about a tree?" Ella got her purple notebook out of her bag. She opened it to the page about the Forbidden City.

"'Find the old pine tree,'" she read
out loud. "'Find the path with three
dragons.'"

Ethan's hazel eyes flashed. "That's it! The tree on this map is a symbol for the old pine tree in the Imperial Garden. If we can find it, then we'll find Grandpa Harry's dragons!"

CHAPTER 5

The Gold Statues

After a few more wrong turns, the twins finally made their way out of the Hall of Supreme Harmony. They blinked in the sunlight and tried to figure out where they were.

They seemed to be in a courtyard. Pigeons fluttered and pecked at the ground. Tourists sat on stone benches or milled around a goldfish pond.

Mr. and Mrs. Briar were not among
them, though.

"I think we should go this way," Ethan said, pointing to a path.

Ella shook her head and pointed to a different path. "I think we should go *that* way. On our map, the skinny path leads to the tree symbol. My path is skinnier than your path."

Ethan shrugged.

They started down the path. They passed several more fancy buildings with red pillars. They also passed a bunch of tour groups. Ella spotted a man with brown hair and glasses in one of them. From a distance, he looked like Mr. Briar!

But when the man turned, Ella's hopes faded. Her dad was wearing his solar system T-shirt, not a shirt with a lion on it.

The twins continued walking. Gradually, the path grew narrower and less crowded. Then it curved to the right. Up ahead was a tiny red house. It reminded Ella of an elf's cottage from a fairy tale.

"What *is* that place?" she wondered out loud.

Ethan strode up to the door and

jiggled the knob. "It's open," he announced. "Let's check it out!"

"Ethan, I don't think we should to go in!" Ella warned him.

"Why not?" Ethan asked.

"We're the only people here. Maybe this part of the Forbidden City is *still* forbidden," Ella said.

"It's fine. Just trust me." Ethan pushed open the door and strolled in.

Sighing, Ella followed. She closed the door behind her.

The twins stopped—and stared.

The tiny red house had only one room inside. The room was no bigger than a closet and glowed with a shimmery light.

Hundreds of little gold statues were perched inside small holes that had been carved into the walls.

"This . . . is . . . so cool," Ethan said at last.

Just then, the door started to open. Someone was coming in!

CHAPTER 6

A Hopeful Surprise

Ethan froze as the door inched open.

He heard a woman's voice. She said something in Mandarin.

"Yes, we must find it!" another woman replied in English.

The twins held their breath. A second later, the door shut. The voices faded away.

"Whew! That was close!" Ethan murmured.

"Too close. We should go. I really don't think we're allowed to be here," Ella said nervously.

"Let's wait until those other people are totally gone," Ethan suggested.

"Okay. But if they come back and we get into trouble, it's your fault!" Ella told him.

Ethan shrugged and turned his attention back to the little gold statues. He recognized tigers, rabbits, and turtles among them.

"Didn't Grandpa Harry say that animals are symbols for different things?" he asked Ella.

Ella nodded. She flipped to the page in her notebook.

"'Dragons equal good luck. Elephants equal strength. Tigers equal courage. Rabbits equal hope.' And

'grasshoppers equal wisdom,'" she
read out loud.

Ethan noticed a whole row of bird
statues. One of the birds looked like a
hawk. He dug through his pockets for
the gold coin that Grandpa Harry had
given him. The coin had an image of
a hawk on it.

"Hey, Ella? Didn't we learn something about hawks in Venice?" he asked.

"Hmm, that does sound familiar." Ella turned to the beginning of her notebook. "Here it is! 'Hawks are messengers of the sky. They also symbolize nobility,'" she read. "If you're noble, that means you come from a very important and powerful family," she added.

"Well, the emperor's family is pretty important and powerful," Ethan said.

"Speaking of families . . ." Ella pressed her ear against the door. "We should keep looking for Mom and Dad. I don't hear those people anymore."

The twins exited the tiny red house. There was no one on the path except for a brown rabbit. It twitched its nose at Ella and Ethan and hopped away into the bushes.

Ella's face lit up. "Hey! Rabbits equal hope!"

"Well, then . . . I *hope* we get to the Imperial Garden soon. I *hope* the dragons give us lots of good luck. And I *hope* Mom and Dad aren't supermad at us," Ethan said.

The rabbit hopped to a tall red gate and disappeared through an opening.

Curious, the twins followed it through the gate.

On the other side was a beautiful

park. Flowers bloomed everywhere. There were temples and pavilions, too.

"Hey, this looks like the Imperial Garden!" Ethan exclaimed.

The twins exchanged high fives.

CHAPTER 7

The Dragons

Ella and Ethan were excited to find the Imperial Garden at last. Now all they had to do was find the old pine tree . . . and the path with the dragons . . . and, most important, their parents!

Ethan spotted a tour group standing outside a small temple. The tour guide was holding a little British flag. *Maybe he speaks English*, Ethan thought.

"Follow me," Ethan told Ella.

"Where?"

"That tour guide. He might be able to help us!"

They rushed over to the group. "Only the emperor and his family were allowed to spend time in the Imperial

Garden," the tour guide was saying. "They sipped tea, played chess, and practiced meditation on these grounds."

The tour guide paused to take questions from the group. Ethan raised his hand. "Excuse me! Is there an old pine tree near here?" he asked.

"Do you mean the four-hundred-year-old pine tree? Just follow this path until you get to a red building called the Hall of Imperial Peace," the tour guide explained. "The tree is right in front. It is known as the Consort Pine, and it symbolizes harmony between the emperor and empress," he added.

The twins thanked the guide and

hurried away. They soon reached the path.

"Look!" Ella cried out.

The path was decorated with statues of different kinds of animals. They were exactly as Grandpa Harry had described!

Ella admired a sculpture of fish swimming in blue waves. It reminded her of the glass mosaic that she and Ethan had found in Venice. Ethan liked the statue of the galloping horses best. There were other animals too.

Now all they had to do was find the three dragons.

A few minutes later, they came

upon the Hall of Imperial Peace.

There was the old pine tree!

Ella had expected it to be tall and straight, like the pine trees they had back home. Instead, the Consort Pine looked like two curvy trees twisting and joining together.

Ethan circled around it. "Here's the path with the dragons!" he announced gleefully.

He and Ella looked up at the sculpture. Three stone dragons—one red, one green, and one purple—breathed fire at one another. Their eyes glowed orange.

"Isn't this awesome?" Ethan said excitedly.

"It's *super*awesome," Ella agreed. "What happens next?"

"I guess we wait for the good luck to happen," Ethan replied.

The twins sat down on a nearby

bench. Five minutes passed. Then another five minutes.

Ella tipped her face to the sky. "Good luck, where are you?" she called out.

Puffy white clouds drifted by. Birds soared through the air.

But nothing happened. Good luck didn't rain down from above. Mr. and Mrs. Briar didn't suddenly appear.

Ella tried to hide her disappointment. "Maybe the dragons don't work anymore."

"Maybe." Ethan seemed pretty disappointed too.

The twins stood up. Ella pointed to

the crinkly old map. "I guess we should head back to the Hall of Supreme Harmony," she said slowly. She didn't know what else to do.

"*Qǐngwèn! Qǐngwèn!*"

Ella turned around. A woman rushed up to them, yelling in Chinese. The woman reached out to grab the map from Ella's hands!

CHAPTER 8

Found!

"Wait!" Ethan shouted as the woman reached for the map.

The woman hesitated. "Oh, you speak English?"

Ethan frowned. Why was the woman trying to steal the map asking them if they spoke English?

"My name is Li Mei. I work at the palace," the woman explained.

"Where did you get that map?"

"We . . . um . . . we found it in the Hall of Supreme Harmony," Ella admitted.

"It was stuck to a man's shoe," Ethan added.

"Oh, thank goodness!" Li Mei

cried out. "This is a very important ancient map of the Forbidden City. A famous archaeologist discovered it just recently."

"An important ancient map?" Ethan said, surprised.

"A famous archaeologist?" Ella said at the same time.

Li Mei nodded. "Yes. There is a special ceremony for it this afternoon. After the ceremony, the map is going into a display in one of our palace museums."

The twins stared at each other and then at the map. They hadn't realized that it was so valuable!

"I wasn't paying attention this morning," Li Mei went on. "All of a sudden, I noticed that the map was

gone. I thought someone had stolen it. But it must have been carried off by the wind."

"I'm glad we found it, then!" Ella said. She handed Li Mei the map.

"Thank you so much! You are quite the detectives!" Li Mei said gratefully. "But are you here by yourselves?" she asked with a concerned look.

Ella shook her head. "We came here with our parents. Our mom's a travel writer. We were supposed to spend today in the Forbidden City as a family. Except . . ."

"We lost them," Ethan finished. "We've been searching for them everywhere."

"Oh dear. I am so sorry. What do they look like?" Li Mei asked.

Ella described her parents.

"Oh! I just saw them in the Palace of Tranquil Peace!" Li Mei said, nodding. "I remember your father's T-shirt," she said with a laugh.

"Can you take us there?" Ethan begged.

"Of course! It is the least I can do for my young detectives who saved the day!"

Li Mei led the twins out of the Imperial Garden. Along the way, they passed the tiny red house from before.

"Hey, Ella! It's the place with the cool gold statues!" Ethan said excitedly.

Ella glared at him.

"What?" Ethan asked, confused.

"We weren't supposed to go inside, remember?" Ella whispered.

"Oh!" Ethan felt his cheeks grow hot.

Li Mei smiled. She didn't seem mad at all. "Those little gold statues

belonged to a long-ago emperor. It was his private collection. That is why they are here instead of in one of palace museums," she explained.

"I have a private collection too!" Ella told Li Mei. "Except I collect shark teeth and seashells."

"How wonderful!" Li Mei said, beaming.

A few minutes later, the three of them reached the Palace of Tranquil Peace. Inside, they saw a big tour group coming out of one of the rooms.

The twins recognized their tour guide from before.

And just behind the tour guide were Mr. and Mrs. Briar!

CHAPTER 9

A Secret Revealed?

Ella and Ethan thanked Li Mei quickly and then slipped quietly to the back of the group.

"How much trouble do you think we're in?" Ethan asked Ella in a low voice.

"I don't know. Probably a *lot*," Ella said worriedly.

Mrs. Briar waved to them just then.

She and Mr. Briar joined them.

"Isn't this a fabulous tour?" Mrs. Briar gushed. "I took so many photos for my column!"

"I'm glad you guys made some new friends," Mr. Briar added.

The twins stared at each other. *Friends?*

Ella glanced around. She saw that they were standing next to a dozen school children in uniforms.

Mr. and Mrs. Briar must have thought the twins had been with the school children all along!

"The tour's almost over. You two must be tired and hungry," Mrs. Briar said.

Ethan grinned at Ella, who grinned back at him. They weren't in trouble after all!

The tour group moved outside. Li Mei stood in the courtyard. She waved to the Briars and rushed up to them.

Ella gulped. Was Li Mei going to

give away their secret to their parents?

"Hello!" Li Mei said to Mrs. Briar. "My name is Li Mei, and I work here at the palace. We are having a special ceremony later for a very old map that was recently discovered. I wanted to invite you and your family

to the ceremony. I heard that you are a travel writer, and I thought you might find the ceremony interesting."

"Oh!" Mrs. Briar looked pleased and surprised. "I didn't realize people here knew who I was. We'd love to come to the ceremony. Wouldn't we, gang?"

"Yes!" Ella, Ethan, and Mr. Briar said at the same time.

Li Mei winked at the twins.

CHAPTER 10

Some Good Luck, After All!

The Briars attended the ceremony that afternoon. A lot of important-looking people gave speeches. Tea with jasmine blossoms was served along with delicious almond cookies. The map the twins had found was displayed in a glass case.

"Well, that was great!" Mr. Briar said after the ceremony was over. They had stopped at a café before leaving the Forbidden City.

"It was very nice of Li Mei to invite us. I still can't believe she knew that I was a travel writer," Mrs. Briar added.

"Yeah," Ella said, nudging Ethan. Ethan nudged her back.

"We'd better get back to our hotel and rest up," Mr. Briar said. "We have a big day tomorrow. We're going to visit the Great Wall. It's more than five thousand miles long! Oh, and tonight for dinner, I thought we could try some fried scorpion."

Fried scorpion? The twins stared at each other in horror.

Li Mei came up to the Briars. "I almost forgot. Here are some souvenirs for your children, from the gift shop," she said, handing Ella and Ethan two white paper bags.

Ella opened her bag. Inside was a little gold statue of a rabbit. Ethan's bag contained a little gold statue of a bird.

"These are copies of statues that a long-ago emperor had in his private collection," Li Mei explained. She winked at the twins again.

"Thank you!" Ella and Ethan said in unison.

"Wow, you kids are pretty lucky!"
Mr. Briar remarked.

The twins smiled. Grandpa Harry had been right after all. The dragons had brought them a whole lot of luck!

GLOSSARY

Hānyíng lai Beijing = Welcome to
                            Beijing

Qǐngwèn = Excuse me

Xièxie = Thank you

*All words are in Chinese.

CHECK OUT THE NEXT

GREETINGS FROM SOMEWHERE

ADVENTURE!

Squaaaawk!

Ethan Briar woke up to a strange noise and glanced around, confused. Where was he? This wasn't his room. The bed was covered with a gauzy gold canopy, not soccer-ball sheets. He didn't recognize the tree growing in the middle of the room or the lantern by his bed either.

His gaze fell on the window. A giant bird perched on the sill opened its long, thin beak.

Squaaaawk!

Ethan let out a yell. He'd never seen such an enormous bird before—at least not up close!

"What's wrong?" Andrew Briar called out from the other bed. He fumbled around for his glasses.

"Dad! There's a pterodactyl in our window!" Ethan exclaimed.

Mr. Briar slipped on his glasses.

"Wow, it's big! No wonder you thought it was from the age of the dinosaurs. I'm guessing it might be a hammer-headed stork. Or a sacred ibis. Wait. Let me look."

He reached over to the tall pile of books on his nightstand. "Okay, here we go. *Birds of Africa.*"

Africa! Ethan nodded to himself, remembering. They were in a lodge in the Maasai Mara National Reserve, which was in Kenya. They had arrived last night along with Ethan's twin sister, Ella, and their mom, Josephine.

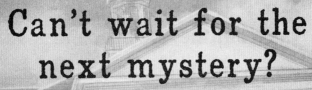

Can't wait for the next mystery?

Find activities, series info, and more.

GREETINGSFROMSOMEWHEREBOOKS.COM